Here's what kids and grown-ups have to say about the Magic Tree House® books:

"Oh, man . . . the Magic Tree House series
is really exciting!"
—Christina

"I like the Magic Tree House series. I stay up
all night reading them. Even on school nights!"
—Peter

"Jack and Annie have opened a door to a world
of literacy that I know will continue throughout
the lives of my students."
—Deborah H.

"As a librarian, I have seen many happy young
readers coming into the library to check out
the next Magic Tree House book in the series."
—Lynne H.

MAGIC TREE HOUSE® #44
A MERLIN MISSION

A Ghost Tale for Christmas Time

by Mary Pope Osborne

illustrated by Sal Murdocca

A STEPPING STONE BOOK™

Random House 🏠 New York

For Jack and Cathy Desroches

Text copyright © 2010 by Mary Pope Osborne
Cover art and interior illustrations copyright © 2010 by Sal Murdocca
Sticker illustrations copyright © 2012 by Sal Murdocca

All rights reserved. Published in the United States by Random House Children's Books, a division of Penguin Random House LLC, New York. Originally published in hardcover in the United States by Random House Children's Books, New York, in 2010.

Random House and the colophon are registered trademarks and A Stepping Stone Book and the colophon are trademarks of Penguin Random House LLC. Magic Tree House is a registered trademark of Mary Pope Osborne; used under license.

Visit us on the Web!
SteppingStonesBooks.com
randomhousekids.com
MagicTreeHouse.com

Educators and librarians, for a variety of teaching tools, visit us at
RHTeachersLibrarians.com

The Library of Congress has cataloged the hardcover edition of this work as follows:
Osborne, Mary Pope.
A ghost tale for Christmas time / by Mary Pope Osborne ; illustrated by Sal Murdocca.
 p. cm. — (Magic tree house ; #44)
"A Stepping Stone book."
"A Merlin mission."
Summary: Jack and Annie travel back to Victorian London when Merlin asks them to use their magic to inspire Charles Dickens to write "A Christmas Carol."
ISBN 978-0-375-85652-5 (trade) — ISBN 978-0-375-95652-2 (lib. bdg.) — ISBN 978-0-375-89467-1 (ebook)
[1. Time travel—Fiction. 2. Magic—Fiction. 3. Brothers and sisters—Fiction.
4. Dickens, Charles, 1812–1870—Fiction. 5. London (England)—History—19th century—Fiction. 6. Great Britain—History—Victoria, 1837–1901—Fiction.]
I. Murdocca, Sal, ill. II. Title.
PZ7.O81167Gh 2010   [Fic]—dc22 2009046171

ISBN 978-0-375-85653-2 (pbk.)

Printed in the United States of America

20 19 18 17 16 15 14 13 12 11

CONTENTS

Dear Reader,

When I was in high school, I spent most of my free time at our town's little theater, acting in plays or working behind the scenes. One year, I was involved in a production of Charles Dickens's <u>A Christmas Carol</u>, a timeless story that readers and theater audiences have enjoyed for over 150 years. After weeks of working backstage, I felt as if I had really visited the exciting, dramatic world of Charles Dickens's Victorian England. One reason I decided to write <u>A Ghost Tale for Christmas Time</u> is that I was eager to revisit that world.

That's the magic of using your imagination: whether you put on a play, write a story, or read a novel, you often end up feeling as if you've actually visited other places, met new people, and shared their adventures. After you finish this book, I hope you'll feel that <u>you've</u> just spent time with Jack, Annie, and Charles Dickens—that you've escaped an angry crowd with them, feasted in an old inn with them, and seen three ghosts with them!

So get ready to wander the twilight streets of London, England, long ago. Horses clomp over the cobblestones, and soon the fog will be rolling in. . . .

Mary Pope Osborne

"There is probably a smell of roasted chestnuts and other good comfortable things all the time, for we are telling Winter Stories—Ghost Stories . . . round the Christmas fire . . ."
—Charles Dickens, from "A Christmas Tree"

Prologue

One summer day in Frog Creek, Pennsylvania, a mysterious tree house appeared in the woods. A brother and sister named Jack and Annie soon learned that the tree house was magic—it could take them to any time and any place in history. They also learned that the tree house belonged to Morgan le Fay, a magical librarian from the legendary realm of Camelot.

After Jack and Annie had traveled on many adventures for Morgan, Merlin the magician began sending them on "Merlin Missions" in the tree house. With help from two young sorcerers named Teddy and Kathleen, Jack and Annie visited four *mythical* places and found valuable objects to help save Camelot.

On their next four Merlin Missions, Jack and Annie once again traveled to *real* times and *real* places in history. After they proved to Merlin that they knew how to use magic wisely, he awarded them the Wand of Dianthus, a powerful magic wand that helped them make their own magic. With the wand, Jack and Annie were then able to find four secrets of happiness to help Merlin when he was in trouble.

Now Merlin wants Jack and Annie to bring happiness to others by helping four creative people give their special gifts to the world. They have already helped the first three—Wolfgang Amadeus Mozart, Louis Armstrong, and Lady Augusta Gregory. Now Jack and Annie are ready to find the last person. . . .

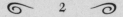

CHAPTER ONE

Did You See That?

Jack and Annie were walking home from soccer practice. It was four-thirty in the afternoon. Sunlight was fading quickly.

"November has really short days," said Jack.

"Yeah, but it has really beautiful skies," said Annie.

The horizon glowed with the orange light of sunset. Suddenly a streak of light blazed over the Frog Creek woods.

"Whoa!" said Jack. "Did you see that?"

"See what?" said Annie.

"A streak of light!" said Jack. "Like a shooting star!"

"Over the woods?" asked Annie.

"Over the woods!" said Jack. He started to run.

"Run!" said Annie.

"I'm running!" said Jack.

Jack and Annie ran down the sidewalk and into the Frog Creek woods. Their feet crunched through fallen leaves as they raced among the shadows. Finally they came to the tallest oak in the woods. The magic tree house sat high in the branches.

Teddy and Kathleen were looking out of the tree house window. The two young enchanters seemed to glow in the fading daylight. Teddy was grinning and waving. Kathleen's long dark hair blew in the breeze.

"Hello!" Teddy called.

"Hello yourself!" Annie shouted back.

"Come up!" called Kathleen.

Jack and Annie hurried up the rope ladder.

They climbed inside the tree house and hugged Teddy and Kathleen.

"We haven't seen you guys in so long!" said Jack. "What have you been doing?"

"Oh, learning more magic—and practicing it," said Teddy. "Turning frogs into boys."

"And boys into frogs," said Kathleen, smiling at Teddy.

"Yes, I rather enjoyed being a frog for a day," said Teddy.

Jack and Annie laughed.

"We missed you!" said Annie.

"We missed you, too," said Kathleen. "We were both delighted when Merlin told us it was time to send you on a new mission."

"Does he want us to help another great artist give their gifts to the world?" asked Jack.

"Yes," said Teddy. "So far you have helped Wolfgang Amadeus Mozart, Louis Armstrong, and Lady Augusta Gregory. Now your mission is to travel to Victorian England and help Charles Dickens."

"His name sounds familiar," said Jack. "But I can't remember why."

"Me neither," said Annie.

"I am sure you will know a great deal about him by the end of your mission," said Kathleen. "In the meantime, here is something to help you." She reached into the folds of her robe and pulled out a book.

The cover showed two girls wearing long skirts and big bonnets. The girls were walking along a path lined with trees. Behind the trees were buildings with towers and tall chimneys.

"London?" said Jack. "That's the city in England where we met William Shakespeare!"

"Yes, but Charles Dickens lived over two hundred years after Shakespeare's time," said Kathleen. "He lived in the 1800s, during Victorian times."

"What's that mean? 'Victorian times'?" asked Annie.

"It means the years during which a queen named Victoria ruled the British Empire," said Teddy.

"Cool, a queen," said Annie. "But can I ask you something? This cover shows girls in long hoop-skirts like I wore when we went to the time of Mozart. It was really hard to run and do stuff in those clothes. Can I please wear something else?"

Teddy laughed. "Yes, I think we can arrange for you to wear more comfortable clothing," he said. "But you may have to pretend to be a boy."

"That's okay," said Annie.

"So do we have a magic instrument for this mission?" asked Jack.

"Indeed," said Kathleen. "We gave you a magic flute to help Mozart, a magic trumpet to help Louis Armstrong, and a magic Irish whistle to help Lady Augusta Gregory. Do you still have the whistle?"

"Sure, we left it here," said Annie. She grabbed the whistle from the corner of the tree house and gave it to Kathleen.

"Thank you," said Kathleen. She tossed the whistle into the air. It spun around and around. There was a flash of blue. The whistle was gone. Floating in its place were a small violin and bow. Kathleen reached up and took them from the air.

"Here is a magic violin to help you on your journey," she said.

"I really like violin music," said Jack.

"Good," said Kathleen. She handed the violin and bow to Jack. "Then on this mission, perhaps *you* should play while Annie makes up a song."

"No problem," said Annie. "And whatever I sing will come true, right?"

"Exactly," said Teddy.

"Any more questions?" asked Kathleen.

"Nope," said Annie.

Jack was sure he had more questions. But before he had time to think of any, Annie pointed to the cover of the book.

"I wish we could go there!" she said.

The wind started to blow.

The tree house started to spin.

It spun faster and faster.

Then everything was still.

Absolutely still.

CHAPTER TWO

Two Gentlemen from Frog Creek

Jack and Annie were both dressed in brown-and-green velvet jackets and dark pants. They wore loose wool caps and shiny new boots. Jack's backpack had become a green velvet bag with a brass buckle.

"Fancy clothes," said Jack.

"Well, at least I'm not wearing a giant skirt, like I wore in Vienna," said Annie.

"Yeah, and these boots aren't full of holes, like the boots we wore in Ireland," said Jack.

"So where did we land?" said Annie. She and Jack looked out the window.

The tree house had landed in a row of big trees. Beyond the trees was a grassy park with gardens and pathways.

Bordering the park was a busy road filled with horse-drawn carriages. Autumn sunlight shone on rooftops, towers, and church steeples. Black smoke rose from hundreds of chimneys.

"London looks great," said Annie. "Let's start looking for Charles Dickens."

"Wait, I'll check the book first," said Jack.

Jack looked in the index of their book and found Charles Dickens. He turned to a page with a photograph of a handsome man with wavy brown hair and huge eyes. Jack read:

Charles Dickens was born in England in 1812. He is one of the most famous writers of all time.

"Of all time?" said Annie. "Wow, he shouldn't be hard to find."

"Maybe he isn't famous yet," said Jack. "If he is, why would he need our help?"

"Good question," said Annie. "Let's start looking for the answer."

"Okay, but first you'd better hide your pigtails," said Jack.

"Oh, right. I'm supposed to be a boy," said Annie. She tucked her pigtails under her cap. "In the past, girls didn't have many choices, did they? How do I look?"

"Fine," Jack said.

"Good, let's go," said Annie.

As Annie climbed out of the tree house, Jack unbuckled the green velvet bag. He put their research book and magic violin and bow inside. Then he buckled the bag and followed Annie down the ladder.

When Jack stepped off the ladder, he heard jingling in his coat pocket. He reached in and pulled out a handful of coins. "Hey, I have money!" he said.

Annie dug into her pockets. "Me too!" she said.

"Great," said Jack. "I didn't like being poor on our last two missions."

Jack and Annie crunched through fallen leaves

until they came to the open park area. A man stood on a platform giving a speech. Women pushed baby buggies. Children sailed toy boats on a pond.

"We have to ask someone for help," said Annie, looking around. "Excuse me!" she called to a woman in a flowery bonnet. "Do you know where Charles Dickens lives?"

"Why, yes, he and his family live at One Devonshire Terrace," the woman said, "below Regent's Park."

"Thanks," said Annie.

"That was easy," said Jack as the woman strolled on.

"I guess he's already famous," said Annie.

"Yeah," said Jack, pulling out their book again. "Let's see if there's a map." He thumbed through the book until he found a map of London. "Here it is. Regent's Park." He looked up. "Where are we now?"

"That sign over there says Hyde Park," said Annie.

"Wrong park," said Jack. He looked at the map again. "Okay. Hyde Park is here . . . and Regent's Park is here. They're pretty far away from each other."

"That's okay," said Annie. "We have money, and London has carriages. This will be fun!"

"Right," said Jack. "Let's go catch a ride."

Jack and Annie hurried over the grass to the busy street bordering the park. Carriages of all shapes and sizes clattered over the cobblestones. Four high-stepping horses pulled an elegant black coach. Two donkeys pulled an old wooden wagon with benches.

"Excuse me!" Jack called to the driver of a small red carriage waiting on the street. "Can you take us to One Devonshire Terrace, below Regent's Park?"

The driver smiled down from his seat. "Indeed, sir!" he said. "I would be proud to carry two fine young gentlemen across our fair city."

Jack caught Annie's eye and smiled. "Thank you," he said.

"Climb into my cab, if you please," said the driver. "Where are you gentlemen from?"

"Frog Creek," said Annie in a deep voice.

"Frog Creek!" said the driver. "Lovely place, I'm sure." Then he flicked the reins, and his fat little horse started clopping up the cobblestone street.

In the cool autumn air, the red cab clattered by toy shops, bootmakers, and hatmakers. The cab passed brick mansions with gardens and ornate buildings with turrets and towers.

"This is a beautiful city," said Annie.

"Yeah," said Jack. He pulled out their book and turned to the beginning. One of the first pages showed a portrait of a plump-faced woman in a red robe. She wore a small crown on her head.

> **The Victorian era in England began when Queen Victoria came to the throne in 1837. She ruled for the rest of the century and helped her country become a powerful world empire.**

"Wow," said Annie. She stuck her head out the

window of the cab and called up to the driver, "Excuse me, sir! Where's the queen today?"

"I believe she's on holiday with Prince Albert," said the driver.

"How long has she been queen?" asked Annie.

"Let's see, she was crowned and moved into Buckingham Palace six years ago," the driver said.

"Thanks!" said Annie. She sat back in her seat. "I love this time in history, with a queen, a prince, and a palace."

"Yep," said Jack. He read on:

During the reign of Queen Victoria, England went through a period known as the Industrial Revolution. People no longer worked mainly on farms. The invention of machines led to work in factories and mines. Many people became very wealthy.

Jack glanced out the window. The people on the sidewalks *did* look wealthy. Women and girls dressed in ruffles and ribbons strolled in and out

of elegant shops. Boys wore frilly white shirts.
Men wore top hats and suits.

Jack read on:

> But while many people became rich in
> Victorian England, many more worked
> under terrible conditions. Even young
> children worked in factories and mines.
> Rich and poor lived side by side, but
> they lived in very different worlds.
> While the rich feasted in grand man-
> sions, the poor often died young of
> hunger and disease.

"Whoa," said Annie. "Maybe I don't love this
time as much as I thought."

The horse and cab came to a halt. "Here we
are!" the driver called. "One Devonshire Terrace."

Jack closed their book and looked up. The cab
had stopped in front of a high brick wall with an
iron gate. Jack and Annie stepped down to the
sidewalk. The driver climbed off of his perch.

"How much do we owe you?" asked Jack.

"One shilling, if you please, sir," said the driver.

Jack reached into his pocket and took out a large coin. He had no idea how much it was worth, but he gave it to the driver. "I hope this is enough," he said.

The man's eyes grew wide. "Why, good heavens, I should say it is! Thank you, gentlemen! Thank you! Thank you! My children thank you! All the good, hardworking people of the world thank you! Shall I come to pick you up later?"

"Sorry, but we don't know how long we'll be here," said Jack.

"Well, perhaps I'll pass by this way now and again," the driver said. "If I see you, I shall certainly stop. I'm always pleased to carry such fine young gentlemen!" The man bowed. Then he climbed back up onto his bench. "Good day, good sirs!" he called, tipping his hat.

As the horse and cab clattered away, Jack looked at Annie. "He was nuts," he said.

Annie laughed. "I think you gave him a lot more than the regular fare," she said.

The gate behind Jack and Annie swung open.

Three small children bounded out to the sidewalk, two girls with curly hair and a round-faced boy.

A woman with a baby followed them out. "Mary! Kate! Charley! Wait for me!"

"Hurry, Mother!" yelled the little boy.

"You wait for me, Charley Dickens!" the young mother called. She caught up with the children, and they all vanished around the corner.

"*Charley Dickens?*" said Jack, stunned.

CHAPTER THREE

Riches to Rags

Jack looked at Annie. "She called that kid Charley Dickens," he said.

"I heard," said Annie. "So Charles Dickens must be five or six years old."

"Oh, man," said Jack, groaning. "So Merlin wants us to help another little kid, like we helped Wolfie Mozart?"

"Seems like it," said Annie.

"Wait a minute. That doesn't make sense. Let's do the math," said Jack. "Our book said Charles Dickens was born in 1812." He pulled out their research book and looked at the first page. "And Queen Victoria became queen in 1837."

"The driver said she's been queen for six years . . . ," said Annie. "So now it's 1843. Subtract 1812 from 1843 . . . ."

Jack squeezed his eyes shut. "And you get . . . thirty-one!" he said.

"Good work!" said Annie.

"So Charles Dickens is thirty-one," said Jack. "And Charley must be Charles *Junior.*"

"Great," said Annie. "Let's go meet Charles Senior."

Jack put away their book, and he and Annie walked to the front gate. Between the iron bars, they could see a beautiful three-story house with tall windows.

"Nice place," said Annie. "It looks like Charles Dickens has already given his gifts to the world."

"Yeah, and gotten some back," said Jack. "So I wonder what his problem is?"

"We'll have to figure that out when we meet

him," said Annie. She jangled a bell hanging from the gate.

A moment later, the front door opened. A stout woman in a white apron came out and walked to the gate. "Yes?" she said through the bars.

"Is this the Dickens residence?" said Annie.

"Yes," said the woman.

"Ah, excellent!" said Annie. "We've come to call on Charles Dickens."

"Indeed? Who are you?" asked the woman.

"We're Jack and An—" started Annie.

"Andrew!" finished Jack.

"Right," said Annie, clearing her throat and deepening her voice. "We're Jack and Andrew from Frog Creek. And who are you?"

"I am Mrs. Tibbs, the housekeeper," said the woman. "And it is my sad job to tell you that Mr. Dickens can have no visitors today. He is working on his latest book and cannot be disturbed."

"Mrs. Tibbs," said Annie, "may we have just five short minutes of Mr. Dickens's time, please?"

"Young man, I am afraid that right now Mr. Dickens needs every minute he can spare for his writing," said Mrs. Tibbs. "Surely you know how important Mr. Dickens's work is."

"Yes, ma'am, surely we do," said Jack. "But—"

"I am terribly sorry, young gentlemen," said Mrs. Tibbs. "It grieves me to turn you away, but I must. I pray that you will bear no grudge against Mr. Dickens." With that, Mrs. Tibbs turned and hurried back inside.

"Well, that didn't get us very far," said Jack.

"Surely it did not," said Annie.

"Pardon us, sirs," someone said.

Jack and Annie turned around.

Two boys with dirty clothes and dirty faces were standing behind them. The taller boy wore an old top hat, and the smaller one wore a wool cap that was too big for him. He carried a large, round brush, a broom, and some rags.

"Oh . . . hi," said Jack.

"We was just needing to ring the bell, sir, if you don't mind," the bigger boy said.

"Sure," said Jack. "But the housekeeper's not letting anyone in today. That's why we're leaving."

"She'll let us in," said the smaller boy. "We've come to sweep the chimneys."

"Really? She'll let you into the house?" said Annie. "Hold on." She turned to Jack. "I've got an idea!"

"No you don't," said Jack. "See you, guys. Bye." He tried to move Annie along, but she pulled away.

"Wait, don't ring the bell yet," Annie said to the boys. "Would you be interested in trading places with us for a while?"

"Annie—" said Jack.

"Shh," said Annie.

The boys looked confused. "Trade places?" asked the bigger boy. "Why?"

"Actually—" said Jack.

But Annie jumped in. "Here's the deal," she said. "We've come a long way. And we really, really want to talk to Mr. Dickens. So . . . maybe if we go in and clean the chimneys, we'll have a chance."

"We can't lose our wages," said the bigger boy.

"How much do you get paid for this job?" asked Annie.

"Twopence," said the smaller boy.

Annie reached into her pocket and pulled out a handful of coins. She gave them to the boy. "Is that good?"

Both boys looked at her with wide eyes and nodded eagerly.

"And you'll get our coats, too," said Annie. "If you give us yours."

"Whoa, whoa. Excuse me," Jack said. He pulled Annie aside. "This is not a good plan."

"Yes it is," Annie said. "Remember when we got kicked out of the Big House in Ireland? If we'd had a job, we could have hung around there longer."

"But we don't know how to sweep chimneys," said Jack.

"How hard can it be?" said Annie. "It will get us inside the house. Then we can keep an eye out for Mr. Dickens. The next thing you know, we've figured out the problem and we're playing our magic music and Mr. Dickens is giving more gifts to the world. Mission accomplished!"

Before Jack could protest, Annie turned back to the chimney sweeps. "So do you want to trade your coats for ours? Hats, too?"

The boys stared at her in wonder. "Them is fine coats, Harry!" said the smaller boy. "And fine hats, too!" He threw down the brush, broom, and rags. He traded his coat for Annie's velvet coat, and traded his dirty, ragged cap for her new, clean cap.

"Hey, you're a girl!" the boy said when he saw Annie's braids.

"So what if I am?" Annie asked, tucking her braids under the dirty cap.

"Forget it, Colin. Rich folks are strange," Harry said. He pulled off his coat and held it out to Jack. "Here," he said with a big grin.

Jack sighed and traded his beautiful velvet coat and wool cap for Harry's tattered coat and old top hat.

"And what about your boots?" asked Harry.

Jack looked down at his shiny leather boots. He looked at Harry's dirty, old shoes.

"Come on, Jack," said Annie. "These guys need them more than we do."

Annie pulled off her boots. Colin took off his shoes and handed them to her. Jack sighed again and sat down to take off his boots.

Colin and Harry stood tall in their new boots and jackets and hats.

"How 'bout it, Colin?" said Harry, shaking his head. "In two minutes, we went from rags to riches."

Colin let out a wild whoop. Then the two boys linked arms and danced a jig, kicking up their boots. When they stopped dancing, Harry rang the gate bell wildly.

As the bell clanged, the front door of the house flew open. The housekeeper stuck her head outside. "Stop the noise, you idiots! I'm comin'!" she screeched.

"Let's go, Colin, before they change their minds!" said Harry.

As the two boys ran off in their new velvet coats, Jack heard money jingling. "Oh, no!" he said. "We forgot to empty our pockets!"

"That's okay," said Annie. "I'm sure they need the money more than we do. They were so happy going from rags to riches."

"Yeah, right," said Jack, "and we just went from riches to rags."

"Shh! Here comes Mrs. Tibbs!" said Annie. "We'd better smudge our faces with the rags so she won't recognize us." She rubbed her face with a dirty rag, then Jack's. "There! You look like a real chimney sweep now."

The housekeeper stomped to the gate and unlocked it. "Don't break my eardrums next time, you knaves!" she cried.

Jack and Annie grabbed the brush and broom. They kept their heads down as they headed for the front door. "Not *that* door, you fools!" yelled Mrs. Tibbs. "Go round to the back!"

CHAPTER FOUR

Out! Out! Out!

Jack and Annie hurried around to the back door and slipped inside the house. They walked through a small, dark mudroom, then stepped into the large front hallway. Sun slanted through the tall windows. Everything seemed to be made of carved wood or marble. A wide staircase curved up to the second floor.

"Get to work, sweeps!" barked the housekeeper. "Do the regular!"

Mrs. Tibbs left them and clomped down the back stairs. Jack heard pots clattering below. He realized the kitchen must be in the cellar. The rest of the house was quiet, as if it were waiting for the mother and children to return.

"I wonder where Mr. Dickens is writing," Annie whispered.

"He must be working quietly somewhere in the house," said Jack.

Mrs. Tibbs came bustling up the back stairs and burst into the front hallway. "I told you to get to work!" she said. "If I don't see you working in two minutes, I'll throw you out on your ears!" The housekeeper then disappeared up the wide staircase to the second floor.

"I guess we'd better get to work," said Jack.

"So where do we start?" said Annie.

"Let's check out the fireplaces on this floor," said Jack.

Jack and Annie crept into a dining room that overlooked a garden. A fire crackled in the hearth.

"She can't expect us to clean *that* chimney," said Jack, "unless she wants us to burn to death."

Jack and Annie went back through the front hall and into a room filled with leather-bound books.

There was no fire in the large fireplace, but the room was bright and warm. It had big windows, a rich-colored plush carpet, and mirrors that reflected the light from outside. A vase of fresh flowers sat on a desk facing one of the windows.

"Oh, man, I love this room," said Jack, staring at all the books.

"Yeah, and look—there's a desk with a feather pen and paper," said Annie. "I'll bet this is where Mr. Dickens does his writing. I wonder where he is."

"Maybe he's taking a break," said Jack.

"Maybe he'll come in here soon," said Annie. "Let's start cleaning the chimney."

"Okay," said Jack. "But first we have to figure out *how*." He unbuckled the green bag and pulled out their research book. He looked in the index and found *chimney sweeps*. He turned to the right page and read aloud:

In Victorian England, young boys worked as chimney sweeps, cleaning the soot made by coal fires. It was not only a dirty job, but a dangerous one as well.

"Great." Jack closed the book. "Good work, Annie. You made us give up our nice clothes and all our money, and you landed us a dirty, dangerous job."

"Don't worry," said Annie. "We shoveled coal, washed dishes, and hauled bananas with Louis Armstrong. We can do this."

"Yeah, but *how* do we do it? The book doesn't tell us," said Jack.

"Well, we've got a brush, a broom, and rags," said Annie. "Let's start by using them. Remember, we're just waiting to run into Charles Dickens. Then we'll chat with him and play our music and—"

"Okay, okay," said Jack. He put the book away.

Jack and Annie stepped into the hearth. Annie got down on her hands and knees and began scrubbing the stones with the brush. Jack pushed his broom up the chimney and tried to sweep the soot off the bricks. A pile of soft black powder fell on his head. It got in his eyes and mouth.

"Oh, no!" whispered Jack, puffing and blowing. As he squeezed his eyes shut, he felt Annie yank his sleeve.

"Don't . . . ," he said. "I—"

"Shh!" whispered Annie. "He's here!"

Jack opened his watery eyes. He saw a small, slender man standing in the hallway outside the door. The man had wavy brown hair. He wore a dark coat and pants. He was reading some papers and muttering to himself.

"Mr. Dickens," whispered Annie.

Before Jack could say anything, the man shouted, "Let no one enter my study, Mrs. Tibbs! Under penalty of death!" And he came into his study and slammed the door.

Penalty of death? thought Jack. *He's got to be kidding!* But he and Annie crouched down in the fireplace.

Mr. Dickens didn't notice them or Jack's green

velvet bag sitting on the carpet. As he crossed the room, he kept looking at his papers and muttering to himself. He sat down at the desk, facing the window. He picked up the feather pen, dipped it into an ink pot, and began to write.

Suddenly Mr. Dickens leapt out of his chair and rushed to one of the mirrors. He put his hands around his neck and cried, "AGHHH!" He struggled and made a horrible face as if someone were choking him.

Then the writer hurried back to his desk and scrawled a few more lines. He stopped and read what he'd written. "Good, good!" he said.

Then Mr. Dickens leapt up again and rushed back to the mirror. This time he rapped his head with his knuckles. He looked furious. "Bah-bah-bah!" he shouted.

Jack and Annie watched, fascinated.

Again Mr. Dickens hurried back to his desk and wrote. He stopped and read what he'd written. Then he crumpled the paper and threw it across the room. He covered his face with his hands and murmured, "I can't, I can't!" He was still for a long moment.

"Excuse me. Are you okay?" Annie asked in a soft voice.

Mr. Dickens gasped and whirled around. He saw Jack's green velvet bag on the carpet. "What's that? Who's here?" Then he saw Jack and Annie huddled in the fireplace. He jumped out of his chair.

"Chimney sweeps?" he cried. "Why—why are you in my study?"

"Sorry, we're just working on the chimney," said Annie.

Mr. Dickens groaned. "I—I can't bear it," he said. "I have to get out. I have to leave. . . ." He rushed across the room and threw open the door.

The housekeeper was sweeping in the hallway. "What's wrong, Mr. Dickens?" she asked.

"I'm finished for today, Mrs. Tibbs," said Mr. Dickens. "They—they . . ." He pointed back into his study.

Mrs. Tibbs saw Jack and Annie. "Oh! What are you doing in there?" she cried. "Mr. Dickens, I'm sorry! They—"

"Never—never mind. I'm going out," said Mr. Dickens. "Tell Mrs. Dickens I don't know when I'll be back." He grabbed his hat and walking stick. Then he hurried out the front door.

"Mr. Dickens, don't go!" cried Mrs. Tibbs. But the door closed before she could stop him.

Mrs. Tibbs whirled around and charged into

the room. "What are you doing in here, filthy brats?" she shrieked. "You know you're to start with the back rooms! Not his study! Never his study!" She waved her broom at them, as if she was trying to sweep them away. "Out! Out! Out!"

Jack grabbed his green bag. Then he and Annie fled from Mrs. Tibbs and her broom. They hurried out the front door.

Mrs. Tibbs followed them to the iron gate. "Poor Mr. Dickens! You've ruined his day!" she cried. "I hope that makes you happy!"

"No, it doesn't," said Annie.

"All of England is waiting for his next story!" cried Mrs. Tibbs.

Oh, brother, thought Jack.

Mrs. Tibbs yanked open the gate. As Jack and Annie tried to slip past her, she grabbed Jack by his jacket. She looked at him closely. "Why, you're not Harry!" She turned and looked at Annie. "And you're not Colin! What have you done with my regular sweeps?" she cried.

"Nothing! They're fine!" said Jack.

"You better not have hurt them, you scamps!" she said, pushing Jack and then Annie out onto the sidewalk.

"They're fine! We promise! We're sorry!" said Annie.

"There's no forgiveness for all the harm you've done today!" the housekeeper said, looking as if she might burst into tears. Then she pushed the iron gate shut. It slammed with a loud *clang!*

CHAPTER FIVE

Stop, Thief!

"Oh, man," said Jack, dazed. "She was nuts. Everyone here is nuts, including Mr. Dickens."

"It's all my fault," said Annie. "I shouldn't have—"

"No, no, don't worry," said Jack. "We just have to catch him and try to fix things."

"He couldn't have gone far," said Annie. She and Jack glanced up and down the busy street. The afternoon sun had disappeared. Dark clouds filled the sky.

"Look, there he is!" said Annie, pointing.

Jack saw Mr. Dickens weaving through the horse-and-carriage traffic. He was signaling to a cabdriver with his walking stick.

"Mr. Dickens!" cried Annie. She started into the street, but Jack grabbed her just in time. Another horse and cab clattered by, barely missing them.

"He's getting away!" said Annie.

"I know," said Jack. "But we don't want to get run over!"

"Look!" said Annie. "There's the driver who brought us here! I'll bet he's waiting for us!"

Across the street was the red cab pulled by the small, fat horse.

"Great!" said Jack. He dodged the carriage traffic and rushed toward the driver. "Hi! Hi there!" Jack yelled. "Thanks for coming back! We need a ride! We have to follow—" He started to climb into the cab.

"Sorry, no free rides today, boy!" the driver said. "I've got mouths to feed at home!" He jiggled his reins, and his horse took off.

Jack nearly fell backward onto the sidewalk.

"Wait! Don't you remember us?" he called. "We're the young gentlemen from Frog Creek!"

But the driver didn't seem to hear him in all the traffic.

Annie touched Jack's arm. "He didn't recognize us. We don't look like gentlemen anymore," she said. "Our clothes are ragged, and we're covered with soot."

"Oh, man," said Jack. "Everyone was nice to us when we looked rich. Now it feels like the whole world's against us."

"I'm sorry, it's all my fault," said Annie.

"Forget it," said Jack. "We just have to find Mr. Dickens. Come on. Let's try to find his carriage."

Clutching his green bag, Jack led the way down the street. He and Annie half ran, half walked past a long row of shops. As they looked for Mr. Dickens, they passed little girls sewing in the window of a dress shop. They saw boys sweeping trash and polishing boots, and girls selling matches and meat pies. Jack had never seen so many kids working at real jobs.

"Hey, isn't that him getting out of that carriage?" said Annie. She pointed to an intersection in the distance.

A small man wearing a top hat and carrying a walking stick was climbing down from a cab.

"Yeah, I think it is!" said Jack. "Hurry!"

Jack and Annie ran up the sidewalk, dodging shoppers and merchants. By the time they got to the intersection, Mr. Dickens had disappeared again.

"Darn," said Annie.

"Let's keep looking," said Jack. "If we don't find him soon, we'll go back to his house and wait for him outside the gate."

A light rain began to fall as Jack and Annie started down a crowded, muddy road. They passed shabby shops and rows of small shacks. They passed vendors selling secondhand clothes and hats and shoes. They saw lots of ragged kids hanging around the street.

Jack caught the eye of a big, tough-looking boy

slouching against a lamppost with his hands in his pockets. As Jack passed him, the boy looked him over. Jack saw the boy say something to another kid. The two of them started walking after Jack and Annie.

"I think we're being followed," Jack said.

"Walk faster," said Annie.

As Jack and Annie hurried up the muddy street, black smoke from chimneys blended with the rain. The air felt grimy and dirty.

Jack glanced back. The two boys were getting closer to them.

"Run!" said Jack.

Jack and Annie ran past a butcher shop, a bakery, and a cigar store. Jack looked over his shoulder. The boys were running, too!

Jack slipped in the mud and fell. Before he could get up, the tough-looking kid caught up with him. The boy grabbed Jack's green velvet bag and took off. The magic violin, the bow, and their book were in the bag!

"Help! Stop him!" cried Jack. "He's got my bag!"

Jack jumped up from the mud and charged after the kid. But the big boy tossed the bag to the other boy.

"That one's got it now!" Annie yelled, pointing.

Jack and Annie took off after the boy with the stolen bag. Fierce anger made Jack run as fast as he could. He caught up with the kid and wrestled the bag away from him. Then Jack turned around and started running back the way they'd come. Annie followed.

"Stop, thief!" the boy yelled.

Jack and Annie kept running through the black rain, passing the same shops again.

"Stop, thief!" Both boys were yelling now. "Stop, thief!"

Thief! Jack thought wildly. Why were they calling *him* thief?

But others quickly joined the two boys, chasing after Jack and Annie:

"Stop, thief!" the butcher yelled.

"Stop, thief!" the baker yelled.

"Stop, thief!" the cigar seller yelled.

Even dogs and old ladies joined the chase through the muddy streets.

Jack looked over his shoulder. The two boys and a bunch of grown-ups and dogs were running after him and Annie. Everyone was yelling, "Stop, thief!"

"What should we do?" cried Annie.

"Keep running," Jack answered. He clutched the green bag closer to his chest and spotted an alley up ahead. "Turn right!" he called.

Jack and Annie ran into the narrow alleyway filled with junk—broken wagon wheels, cracked plates, old pots and pans. The crowd followed them down the alley. Everyone kept shrieking, "Stop, thief!"

As the black rain fell, Jack and Annie scrambled over the rubble, desperately looking for an escape. Soon they came to a dead end. There was nowhere else to run!

Jack and Annie turned around. The crowd was closing in on them. Jack clutched the green bag in his hand. "Get away from us!" he shouted. "This is my bag! It's mine!"

But the crowd kept moving toward him, led by the two boys who'd stolen the bag. They sneered at Jack. "We've got you now, thief," said one.

"Just hand the bag over to us," said the other, "or we'll have to take it."

"Play the violin, Jack!" said Annie.

Of course! thought Jack. Only magic could save them now! Jack turned his back to the crowd. But before he could unbuckle the bag, someone grabbed him by his shirt collar. Jack looked up.

A large man wearing a blue uniform loomed over him. "I'll take that bag, boy," the policeman said, holding out his hand.

CHAPTER SIX

To Jail

Jack handed the policeman his green bag. "But it's mine, sir!" he tried to explain. "I promise it's mine!"

"No, it's mine!" said the kid who'd stolen the bag. "It belonged to my dear, departed father."

"It is not yours!" Jack said, furious.

"It is!" the boy shouted. "Take him to jail, Officer!"

"Stand back!" the policeman shouted at the kid. "Don't worry, I will be puttin' him in jail. But I might be puttin' you there, too!"

"Jail?" said Jack.

"But, sir, it really *is* our bag," said Annie. "Those two kids stole it from us, and my brother just grabbed it back and—"

"Quiet!" the policeman said. "Someone stole it—whether it's *him* or *him*, or maybe *you*, we'll soon find out."

"But I can tell you what's in it!" said Jack. "I can prove—"

"Quiet! You can make your case to the chief inspector at Scotland Yard!" said the policeman. "Step aside! Let us through!" he yelled at the crowd.

As the crowd parted to make a path, Jack saw the tough kid and his friend slip away down the alley. "They're running away, sir!" he said.

But the policeman ignored him. "March!" he ordered.

Annie grabbed Jack's hand and walked close to him. "I'm sorry," she said, near tears. "I'm so sorry I made us give up our nice clothes."

"Don't worry," said Jack. "You didn't know this

would happen." He wasn't mad at Annie. He was mad at the boys who had tried to steal his bag. And he was mad at Merlin, Teddy, and Kathleen! Why had they sent him and Annie to such a terrible place? He didn't care at all about helping crazy Mr. Dickens anymore. He just wished they were back home in Frog Creek.

"This way!" the policeman ordered. He gave Jack a little push. Jack and Annie turned out of the alley and headed down the street. They walked through the smothering coal smoke and grimy rain.

"Left!" the policeman shouted.

Jack and Annie turned left. The crowd still followed them. Jack kept his head down. He couldn't bear to look at the gawkers.

"Hello!" Annie suddenly shouted. "It's us! Remember us?"

Jack looked up. Who was Annie shouting to?

Standing on the other side of the street was Mr. Dickens.

"It's us!" Annie called again. "The chimney

sweeps in your study! Remember?"

Mr. Dickens scowled, but he started to follow them, walking behind the crowd.

"Help us!" Annie shouted. "Please help us!"

"Quiet, boy!" the policeman barked at Annie.

Mr. Dickens moved briskly toward Jack and Annie, pushing his way through the crowd. "Excuse me, Officer!" he said.

The policeman stopped. He squinted at the small, well-dressed man. "Mr. Dickens? Mr. Charles Dickens?" he said with wonder.

Gasps and whispers went up from the crowd. "It's him. It's Charles Dickens, the writer!" the baker said.

"Yes, it is I," said Mr. Dickens. "I know these sweeps. What seems to be the problem, Officer?"

"The boy stole this bag, sir." The policeman held up the green velvet bag.

"When? When did he steal that bag?" asked Mr. Dickens.

"Just now, sir. I caught him trying to run off with it," said the policeman.

"Well, I'm afraid you're mistaken, Officer," said Mr. Dickens. "These lads were working at my house earlier today. They had that green bag with them then."

"Ah, did they now?" said the policeman, looking at Jack.

Jack nodded.

"This lad is innocent," said Mr. Dickens. He turned and spoke to the crowd. "Do you see what has happened here? If I had not come along, the courts might have thrown this boy in jail for years. Why? Because he has soot on his face and holes in his shoes. How do you think this lad got so dirty? I ask all of you!"

No one in the crowd answered.

"I'll tell you how," said Mr. Dickens. "From honest work. And now all of you want to put this innocent, hardworking lad into prison?"

The butcher, the baker, and the cigar seller lowered their gazes. The policeman looked ashamed, too. "Mr. Dickens, forgive me. I shall release him at once," he said.

"Yes, Officer, release this lad. Return his bag, and think twice before you arrest another child just because he is ragged and poor," said Mr. Dickens.

The policeman handed the green velvet bag to Jack. "Your bag, boy," he said. "Good luck on your journey through life. God bless you. And God bless you, Mr. Dickens. Good day."

"Thank you, Officer. And one last word to all of you," Mr. Dickens said to the crowd. "Remember, goodness dresses in rags and patches as often as it dresses in velvet and silk."

The crowd was silent for a moment. Then some people broke into applause.

Mr. Dickens tipped his hat. He put his hands on Jack's and Annie's shoulders. "Come, lads. I will walk with you a ways, so no one else will prey upon you," he said.

"Thanks," Jack said hoarsely.

Mr. Dickens guided Jack and Annie away from the crowd. He steered them across the street.

"Thanks for helping us," said Annie. "We're sorry we ruined your work today. We didn't mean to."

"Oh, no, you didn't ruin my work," said Mr. Dickens. "It was just that the sudden sight of you reminded me of all the children who sweep our chimneys and work in our mines and factories. You suffer. . . ." He shook his head. Then he looked at them and tried to smile. "Forgive me, lads. I needn't tell you about your own hard lives. Instead, you both must tell me about yourselves."

"Well, first, I'm not a lad," said Annie. "I'm a girl. My name is Annie." She took off her cap, and her pigtails fell to her shoulders.

Mr. Dickens's big eyes grew bigger. "Why, I am speechless!" he sputtered.

Annie shrugged. "Sorry, Mr. Dickens, but this is the real me."

"Well—well, *Annie*, I'm delighted to meet the real you!" Mr. Dickens looked at Jack. "And are you also a little girl in disguise?" he asked.

"No!" said Jack. "I'm her brother, Jack."

"I see," said Mr. Dickens. "So you are Jack and Annie. Well! I would like it if you both called me Charles."

"Thank you, Charles," said Annie.

"So now, Jack and Annie, what exactly happened today with the policeman and the mob?" asked Charles.

"Tell him, Jack," said Annie.

"No, *you* tell him," said Jack. He felt too upset to talk about it.

"Okay, Charles, I'll tell you," said Annie.

As Annie told the story of how the boys had stolen the bag, Charles listened carefully, nodding and frowning. His eyebrows jumped up and down. His mouth twitched. He seemed to be feeling everything Annie was describing.

Finally Annie finished, saying, "And then you came, and you know the rest."

"Remarkable!" said Charles.

"Yes, it was remarkable," Jack said bitterly.

"No, it *is* remarkable because it is exactly like a scene in my book *Oliver Twist*!" said Charles. "Oliver is wrongly accused of picking the pocket of an old man. And the real thieves lead the chase, yelling, 'Stop, thief!'"

"Really?" said Jack.

"Are you serious?" said Annie. "That happens in your book?"

"Indeed," said Charles.

"Cool," said Jack with a little smile.

"Does that make you feel better?" Annie asked Jack.

"Yeah, it does, actually," he said. "It makes me feel like I'm not alone."

"Good!" said Charles. "Now, tell me, Jack and Annie, are you hungry?"

Jack and Annie nodded.

"Of course you are!" said Charles. "I imagine you've had nothing but watery gruel for days! Let me treat you to a meal that you will never forget! Steak and gravy! Pork pie! Gooseberry jam! Come, we will dine like kings!" He looked at Annie. "And a *queen*!" he added with a wink.

CHAPTER SEVEN

Bah, Humbug!

Night was falling as Charles led Jack and Annie across the street to an old inn. Candles twinkled in the paned windows. Charles ushered them through the door and into a warm dining room. The room had low ceilings with dark wooden beams. A fire crackled in a huge fireplace at one end.

"Ah, Mr. Dickens, welcome! Welcome!" said a man with a pointed nose and small eyes. He bowed low and rubbed his hands together.

"Thank you, Mr. Pinch," said Charles.

"What brings you to my humble inn today?" Mr. Pinch asked.

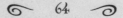

"I've come to dine with my two friends, Mr. Pinch," said Charles.

The innkeeper looked down at Jack and Annie. He frowned at their ragged, muddy clothes. *"These* are your friends, Mr. Dickens?" he said. He wrinkled his nose as if he smelled something bad.

"Yes. They are hardworking children," said Charles. "And they are quite hungry."

"I see. . . ." Mr. Pinch looked fretfully around the room. "Well, what about that table in the corner, Mr. Dickens?"

"Yes, Mr. Pinch, that will be fine," said Charles.

Mr. Pinch ushered them to the table. A waiter brought them silverware and lit a candle. Some of the diners began to notice Charles Dickens and whispered to one another.

An elegantly dressed couple came over to the table. "Excuse me, Mr. Dickens," the woman said shyly. "But I want you to know how much my husband and I love your stories."

"Why, thank you!" said Charles, grinning. "Tell me, what do you love most about them?"

As the couple began talking about their favorite scenes from his books, more people gathered around Charles Dickens.

At the same time, serving people delivered heaping plates of food to the table: baked apples, turkey drumsticks, steak pie, mashed potatoes, brown bread, buttery cheese, dark jam, and steaming cups of tea. Jack and Annie started to eat at once. Gobbling his mashed potatoes, Jack noticed that Charles Dickens didn't even look at his food. He was too busy laughing and talking with his fans.

People all over London love Charles, Jack thought. *So why did Merlin send us here?* So far Charles was only helping *them*. They weren't helping *him* at all.

"Jack, look," Annie whispered. She pointed toward a window.

A man and a small boy were staring through the glass, their faces lit by candlelight. The man was leaning on a crutch. He and the boy were both thin and sad-looking.

"They're staring at Charles," Jack mumbled, his mouth full of potatoes.

"No, I think they're staring at our food," said Annie.

While Charles kept talking with his fans, Annie took a drumstick, two pieces of bread, and a chunk of cheese from her plate. She wrapped them in a napkin. Then she slipped away from the table and out the door of the inn.

Mr. Pinch cried out. He waved his hands and charged to the door. He yelled in a shrill voice, "Come back here, urchin! Where are you going with that?"

Oh, no, not again! thought Jack. He leapt up and ran to the doorway. He pushed past Mr. Pinch and stepped outside into the chilly air.

Annie was standing with the little boy and the man with the crutch. She was offering them her bundle of food.

"Don't you dare give that food away!" cried Mr. Pinch.

"Why?" said Jack. "She's not stealing anything. She's giving them some of her own dinner."

"What is happening here?" said Charles, stepping outside.

The little boy grabbed the bundle of food from Annie. "Thank you," he said softly, and he and the man took off. The man's crutch thumped on the pavement as he hobbled away with the boy.

"That's right! Get out of here!" Mr. Pinch yelled after them. "No greedy mice begging at my inn! And you, urchin, you had no right to do that!"

"Mr. Pinch, from what I could tell, my young friend was only showing compassion," said Charles.

"Bah! Foolishness!" said Mr. Pinch. "Rumors will spread now that I give away food!"

"And what harm would come of that?" Charles asked the innkeeper. "You're rich enough. You can afford to share a bit with those less fortunate."

"Bah, humbug!" said Mr. Pinch. "Are there no poorhouses to feed them? No workhouses? Let them eat in debtors' prisons! The father should put the boy to work! There are plenty of factories that would hire him!"

Charles seemed unable to speak as he stared at the stingy man.

"Charles?" said Annie.

Jack didn't know what was wrong with Charles. But he knew he should get him away from the miserable innkeeper. "Let's leave," he said, tugging on Charles's sleeve. "Let's go."

Charles looked at Jack. "Yes . . . yes . . . ," he said absently. "Indeed."

"Wait a second," said Jack. He dashed back into the warm dining room and grabbed his green velvet bag. On his way out, he noticed that everyone had gone back to their dinners. They were eating and talking, their lives untouched by the sad events outside.

Jack joined Charles and Annie on the street. "All set," he said.

"Mr. Dickens? Please!" Mr. Pinch whined from the doorway. "Pay me before you leave? Please, sir?"

"Yes. Yes . . . of course." Charles pulled out his wallet and paid the innkeeper.

Mr. Pinch smiled. "You understand, don't you, sir?" he said. "It's not my job to feed all of England."

"No. Of course it isn't," said Charles. Then he walked away from the inn. Jack and Annie followed him.

It was colder and darker now. Brownish fog shrouded the street. A lamplighter was lighting the streetlamps.

"Are you okay, Charles?" asked Annie.

Charles barely nodded. "Yes—uh—did you children get enough to eat?" he said.

"Yes, thank you," said Annie. "We're fine. But are you all right?"

"Me?" He let out a long, shaky sigh. "Sorry, but I—I must leave you now," he said. "Here." Charles pulled out his wallet again. "Take this. I want you to buy new boots and a week's worth of food. I'm sorry to leave you, but I must." His hands shook as he held out the leather wallet.

"No, we can't," said Jack.

"I insist," said Charles, giving him the wallet. "Thank you for your company. And bless you both." Charles Dickens then walked away from them, disappearing into the brown fog.

CHAPTER EIGHT

A Terrible Story

"What do you think is wrong with him?" said Annie.

"I don't know," said Jack. He put the wallet in his bag. "But so far our mission's been a disaster."

"Well, we can't give up now," said Annie. "Come on, let's follow him."

As Jack and Annie started after Charles, the street was quiet and empty. It seemed the blinding fog and damp drizzle had driven everyone inside.

They hadn't gone far before Charles looked back and saw them. "Don't follow me, children!"

he called. "Please! I want to be alone now! I must be alone."

Jack and Annie watched Charles vanish into the mist.

"Maybe we should go back," Jack said. "We could find our way to his house and wait for him there."

"Something tells me he's not going home soon," said Annie. "I feel like he really needs our help *now*."

Jack sighed. "Yeah, I feel that way, too," he said. "So let's follow him. But we'd better keep a safe distance from him, so he doesn't see us."

As Jack and Annie followed Charles through the fog, they could hear the tapping of his walking stick on the cobblestones. They followed the sound down a sloping street lined with shacks.

In the dingy light of the gas streetlamps, Jack could see garbage in the gutters—cabbage leaves, moldy bread, rotten fish. The poor neighborhood frightened him. But he and Annie kept going, following the sounds of Charles's footsteps and the tapping of his walking stick.

Then the sounds stopped.

"Wait," Jack whispered.

Jack and Annie froze. They couldn't see Charles through the fog, but they could hear the sound of sobbing.

"Oh, no!" whispered Annie.

Jack and Annie moved closer to the sound. Charles was sitting under a streetlamp at the bottom of the hill. His head was resting in the crook of his arm.

"Charles?" said Annie. She stepped closer to Charles. "Are you okay?" Annie sat on the curb next to him.

Jack sat on the other side of Charles. "You want to talk about it?" he asked.

Charles lifted his head. "I'm sorry. I've never told anyone this story before," he said. "Not even my wife or my closest friends."

"You can tell us," said Jack.

Charles looked at Jack, then at Annie. He stood and motioned for them to join him. Then he pointed into the fog. "Over there, near the river, was once a shoe polish factory. It was a tumble-down old building, filled with river rats. I went to work there when I was twelve. I sat at a table, pasting labels onto pots of black polish. I worked eleven hours a day, six days a week, yet I barely earned enough to keep alive."

"You were only twelve?" said Jack.

"Yes. And I lived alone. I had lost everything—my family, my school, my dignity," said Charles.

"Were you an orphan?" asked Annie.

"No. I had parents," said Charles.

"Why did they make you work in such a bad place?" asked Jack.

"My father had fallen on hard times," said Charles. "He was a good man, but he couldn't pay his bills. So he was sent to a debtors' prison across the river. My mother chose to live there with him."

"That's a terrible story," said Annie.

"Wait a minute," said Jack. "You mean your dad was sent to prison because he couldn't pay his bills?"

"Yes," said Charles.

"That doesn't make sense," said Jack. "How could he earn the money to pay his bills if he was in prison?"

"That's a very good question," said Charles.

"That doesn't happen anymore," said Jack, thinking of life back in Frog Creek.

"Oh, yes, it does," said Charles. "Life is still

miserable for thousands of poor. Parents live in prisons and workhouses, while countless children work in factories and mines for pennies."

"But at least things are different for *you* now," said Annie. "You're a famous writer. That should make you feel better."

"How can that make me feel better?" said Charles. "What is writing? Just ink on a page. It's not food for the hungry. It's not medicine for the sick. Lately I've been thinking I should give up my writing altogether."

"Oh, no," said Jack. "You can't do that."

"It seems so foolish and vain," said Charles.

"But—" said Jack.

"No," said Charles. He let out a shuddering sigh. "I have decided: I shall write no more."

"Charles, what about—" said Annie.

"Be kind, children, and leave me now," said Charles. "I need to be alone. My heart dies inside of me."

"Oh. Okay . . . ," said Annie. She and Jack stood up. "Bye, Charles . . ."

Jack started to wish Charles good luck, but the words stuck in his throat. There was really nothing to say. As Charles covered his face in despair, Jack and Annie started back up the hill.

"We can't just leave him," said Jack.

"I know. So let's stay nearby," said Annie.

Jack and Annie found a stoop to sit on, and they watched over the lonely figure at the bottom of the hill.

"Now I know why Merlin sent us here," said Jack. "But this really seems hopeless."

"Look in our research book," said Annie. "Maybe it can help us."

Jack pulled out their book and looked up Charles Dickens again. He read aloud:

Charles Dickens was born in England in 1812. He is one of the most famous writers of all time. He wrote many novels, including *Oliver Twist, A Christmas Carol,* and—

"Wait, wait," said Annie. "*A Christmas Carol?*

Wasn't that the name of the play we saw last year with Mom and Dad and Grandma?"

"Yeah," said Jack, "on Christmas Eve. Oh, man, that's why the name *Charles Dickens* sounded familiar."

"Look, there's a picture of Scrooge, the mean guy in the play," said Annie. She pointed to a picture in the book. It showed an old man wearing a nightcap and holding a candle.

Jack read the caption underneath:

> **A Christmas Carol has been retold again and again in plays, movies, and television shows. To this day, it inspires people to be kinder and more generous to others.**

"Wow, remember the three ghosts who visit Mr. Scrooge?" said Jack. "The Ghost of Christmas Past, the Ghost of Christmas Present, and the Ghost of Christmas Future."

"Right. They try to change him by showing him his past, his present, and his future," said Annie.

"At the end of the story, he's like a different person. I can't believe Charles wrote that story!"

"Well, now it seems like he won't," said Jack. "He just said he's never going to write again. He said his heart has died."

Annie stood up and brushed herself off. "So get out the violin and the bow," she said matter-of-factly.

"Oh, I forgot all about our magic violin!" said Jack.

"Me too, until now," said Annie. "Get it out. I'll make up a song."

"What kind of song?" asked Jack.

"I'll make up my own version of *A Christmas Carol*," said Annie. "But it won't be a story about Scrooge. It'll be a story about Charles—a *ghost* story about Charles Dickens."

CHAPTER NINE

The Three Ghosts

"A ghost story?" said Jack. "You mean we'll make ghosts appear?"

"Yep," said Annie.

"Um . . . I don't know," said Jack. Ghosts made him nervous.

"I promise this will work," said Annie.

"But I don't get it," said Jack. "A ghost story. How can we change Charles with that?"

"*We* won't change him. The *ghosts* will change him, just like they changed Scrooge," said Annie. "Our job is just to make the right ghosts appear."

"But—" started Jack.

"It's *magic*, Jack," said Annie. "We have to trust the magic."

"But Charles doesn't even want us around," said Jack.

"That's okay," said Annie. "He doesn't have to see us. He can believe it's all happening in his imagination. He has a great imagination, you know. Come on, before he leaves."

Jack sighed. "Okay," he said. "But I hope we don't give him a heart attack." He unbuckled the green velvet bag and pulled out the violin and the bow.

Jack rested the bow against the strings of the violin. Then he began moving the bow back and forth. The violin's music was soft at first, but as it grew louder, it seemed to come from every direction.

At the bottom of the hill, Charles lifted his head.

Annie started singing in a soft, whispery voice:

Come, three ghosts,
in a dreamlike swirl.
Help our friend
give his gifts to the world.

The streetlamp flickered and went out. Then a hazy glow surrounded Charles. He stood up and looked around. In the haze, a ghostly figure swirled into shape.

Jack's heart pounded as he kept playing.

Charles cried out and stumbled back.

The ghost looked like both a child and an old man. He had long white hair, but there was not a wrinkle on his face. He wore a white tunic with a silver belt and carried a holly branch in his hand.

Annie sang on:

Do not fear him, Charles,
stand fast.
He's come to share
a Christmas Past.

The ghost waved his hand, and a scene slowly appeared in the glowing fog: a small, frail boy was lying on a heap of rags.

"Who are you? And why do you show me this poor child?" cried Charles.

The boy rolled over and sat up. He had big eyes and wavy brown hair.

Charles gasped. "Oh, my!" he said. "Is that . . . is that *me*?"

The boy reached under the rags and pulled out a book. On the cover was a picture of a flying carpet. The boy opened the book and smiled.

"I remember that book! It *is* me!" cried Charles. "I loved to read *The Arabian Nights*! I felt as if I could ride on a flying carpet myself! Books gave me hope when I had no hope. But why do you show me this now?"

The ghost did not answer. He raised his pale hand in farewell.

"Wait!" cried Charles.

But the ghost faded into the haze. And the vision of young Charles Dickens faded with him.

The glow still surrounded Charles. Jack's violin music swelled with deep tones. Annie sang on.

Come to Charles,
O second ghost.
It's your turn now
to be the host. . . .

The haze became rose-colored. It swirled in the shape of a small cyclone. The funnel of vapor spun wider and wider, until out from its center stepped a giant in a green robe. He had a bushy brown beard and wore a crown of icicles. He held a flaming torch high into the air.

"Who are you? What do you want with me?" cried Charles.

The ghost pointed into the mist and bellowed:

> *You say you'll write*
> *not one more book?*
> *Stop your weeping, man,*
> *and look!*

Charles stared as human shapes began to form in the mist: a young Victorian couple stood at a bookstall. "I'm getting the new book by Charles Dickens! I love Mr. Dickens!"

"I know you do, my dear! And so do I!"

The couple laughed joyfully, and another scene appeared beside them: a teacher stood in front of schoolchildren. "So what did we learn today from Mr. Dickens's book?" she asked.

"We learned to be more generous and kind!" a small girl answered.

"Yes!" the class shouted.

As the children cheered, another scene took shape: Queen Victoria was sitting on her throne!

"I say," the queen said to a lady-in-waiting. "This *Oliver Twist* book is exceedingly interesting. Poor Oliver. I had no idea children in our kingdom lived such dreadful lives."

The queen faded away. The couple faded away—and the teacher and the children. Everything faded away except the giant ghost.

"They were all speaking about my books," Charles said in a voice filled with wonder.

The giant ghost boomed:

> *Yet writing is nothing*
> *but paper and ink!*
> *A foolish task!*
> *Is that not what you think?*

"Yes! No! Yes, but . . . ," said Charles.

The ghost shook his head sadly. Then he, too, vanished into the fog.

Annie sang on:

> *Think about all*
> *you've been shown by this ghost,*
> *and get ready to meet*
> *your last ghostly host.*

The rosy glow faded to an eerie silver light. The air grew very cold. Then, like a dark shadow, a third ghost silently appeared. This ghost wore a black cape with the hood pulled over its head.

Charles raised his walking stick to protect himself. Jack trembled with cold and fear, but he kept playing the violin.

The ghost glided slowly toward Charles.

"Who are you? What do you want?" Charles cried.

A scene swirled into view beside the ghost: a group of people stood in a graveyard. A young woman was weeping near a tombstone.

"Why—why do you show me this scene of grief?" asked Charles.

The ghost pointed a bony finger at the tombstone.

Charles lowered his walking stick and crept

closer. He squinted at the writing on the tombstone. He gasped. "It's *my* name!" he cried. "My
name is on that stone!"

"Poor Papa," the young woman said to the other mourners. "How sad that he stopped writing when he was so young. So many beautiful words might have been written. So many wonderful characters might have lived. If only he'd given more stories to the world, he might have touched the hearts of millions." The woman broke down in tears again.

"Stop! Stop!" cried Charles. "I can't bear it!"

The scene began to fade.

"Wait!" Charles shouted to the ghost. "I've changed my mind! Tell her I *will* keep writing! Wait!"

But the ghost and the mourners and the tombstone had already disappeared into the fog. Charles Dickens stood alone in the cold silver light.

Jack played one long, low note on the magic violin.

Then there was silence.

CHAPTER TEN

A Christmas Carol

The gas streetlamp flickered back on. Charles began pacing back and forth.

"Come on, Jack," said Annie. "Let's go talk to him! Quick!"

Jack packed up the violin and bow. Then he and Annie hurried down the hill to Charles.

"Charles!" cried Annie. "Hello!"

Charles whirled around. "Annie! Jack! You can't imagine what just happened!" His voice was shaking. "I had the strangest visions! Three ghosts came to me! They showed me visions of myself

in the past, the present, and the future!"

"Really?" said Annie. "That sounds like a scene in a book."

"Yes, yes, it certainly does!" Charles said, laughing and wiping his eyes. "The ghosts made me want to keep writing. They taught me that I can truly help the world with my books! I—I must go home! I must find a cab and go home and get to work at once! I cannot waste another day! Another hour! Another minute! I must write! I love to write!" He laughed with joy.

"Then I guess we'll be going home, too," said Jack, smiling. "Our job is done here."

"Shall I tell the cab to let you off somewhere?" asked Charles.

"We need to go to Hyde Park," said Annie.

"Wonderful! It's on the way. Come along!" said Charles. He took off running up the hill, dashing ahead of Jack and Annie. When they caught up with him, they saw a horse and cab clattering over the cobblestones.

"Stop, sir! Give us a ride, please!" Charles shouted to the driver.

The driver brought his horse to a halt. Jack and Annie followed Charles to the cab. "Hyde Park! Then One Devonshire Terrace! Please hurry!" said Charles.

The driver looked delighted. "Yes, Mr. Dickens, sir!" he said.

The three of them crowded into the cab, and the horse began to trot through the dark, foggy city, its hooves clopping on the cobblestones.

"Ah!" said Charles, clapping his hands. "I know now what I shall write about! I will write a Christmas story about a man whose life is changed by three ghosts! The Ghost of Christmas Past! The Ghost of Christmas Present! And the Ghost of Christmas Future! What do you think of that?"

"It sounds brilliant," said Jack.

"I agree!" said Charles. "I'll write about a greedy, selfish man who helps no one. Like—like Mr. Pinch! But I'll call him—what shall I call him?"

"How about Scrooge?" said Annie.

"Wonderful name!" Charles laughed. *"Mr. Scrooge!* I love it. The three ghosts will change Scrooge's life! Do you like that idea?"

"Love it," said Jack.

"Good!" said Charles. "I think I shall just be able to write the story in time for Christmas. Hah! Perhaps I'll call it *A Ghost Story of Christmas.*"

"Hmm. Or maybe you could just call it *A Christmas Carol,*" said Jack.

"Oh! I love that!" said Charles. "Yes, perhaps I'll call it *A Christmas Carol.* And then underneath those words, I'll write: *Being a Ghost Story of Christmas!*"

"That sounds good," said Annie.

"That should make people want to read it," said Charles. "Everyone loves a ghost story, don't they?"

"Well . . . ," started Jack.

"Of course they do!" said Charles. "It all makes sense to me now. I will keep using my books to fight greed and cruelty. My pen is my sword. Except my books will never celebrate wars and fighting. They'll always show the joys and sorrows of real people. They'll show how good always triumphs over evil."

"Great," said Jack.

Charles sat back in his carriage seat and chuckled, his eyes shining in the lamplight. "I'm as light as a feather, as happy as an angel. Am I not the luckiest man on earth?"

"I think you might be," said Annie.

The horse came to a stop. "Hyde Park, Mr. Dickens, sir," the driver called down.

"Well, Jack and Annie, I hope you have enjoyed your time with me. I trust I have been of some help to you," said Charles. He sounded like the old Charles, pleased and proud of himself.

Jack didn't mind. A happy Charles was much better than a sad one.

"Yes," said Jack. "But we have to give this back to you." He pulled out the leather wallet that Charles had given them. "Thanks, but we don't need it."

"Oh, no, please keep it," said Charles. "Buy food with the money. Buy boots. Buy books!"

"Actually, we have lots of books," said Jack. "And we have food at home and shoes and parents. We have everything we need."

"Charles, please share it with others who aren't so lucky," said Annie.

"Why, I don't know what to say," said Charles. "You two are the most extraordinary children I've ever met. Clearly you have good, generous hearts. You already live the message I want to write in *A Christmas Carol*."

Annie smiled. "Yeah, well, it's always good to be reminded," she said. "I can't wait to read your story."

"And where will you go now?" asked Charles. "Will you be safe?"

"Yes, our parents take good care of us," said Jack. "You don't have to worry."

"I shall never forget you," said Charles.

"We won't forget you, either," said Annie. "Good-bye, Charles."

Jack and Annie hopped down from the cab and took off through the park. The fog was so thick it was impossible to see the tree house. Jack couldn't even see Annie. He was relieved when she called out, "I found it!"

Jack ran toward the sound of Annie's voice. She was already halfway up the ladder. As he started up after her, church bells began to bong, striking the hour.

Jack and Annie climbed inside the tree house and looked out the window. But there was nothing to see, nothing except the heavy fog.

"Charles is going to be fine," said Annie.

"Yep," said Jack with a smile. "He never even knew that it was us who helped him."

"That's the best way to help someone, I think," said Annie.

"Why?" asked Jack.

"Then you know you're not helping them just to get a lot of credit," said Annie. "You're helping because it's the right thing to do."

Jack nodded. What Annie had just said felt true. "Ready to go home now?" he said. He picked up the Pennsylvania book.

Annie nodded.

Jack pointed to a picture of the Frog Creek woods. "I wish we could go home," he said.

The wind began to blow.

The tree house started to spin.

It spun faster and faster.

Then everything was still.

Absolutely still.

CHAPTER ELEVEN

Gifts to the World

No time at all had passed in Frog Creek. The sky was lit by the orange afterglow of the sunset. Jack and Annie were wearing their jeans and jackets and sneakers again. The green velvet bag had changed back into Jack's backpack.

"Jack! Annie!" two voices called from the woods below.

Jack and Annie looked out the window. Teddy and Kathleen stood in the shadows beneath them!

"Hi! Hi!" Annie and Jack called. They quickly climbed down the rope ladder and hopped to the ground.

"We're glad to see you!" said Annie. "Why are you here?"

Before Teddy or Kathleen could answer, the leaves rustled, and out from the dark trees stepped Morgan le Fay and Merlin the magician.

"Morgan! Merlin!" said Annie.

Peep.

"Penny!" said Jack.

Waddling behind Merlin was the baby penguin Jack and Annie had given to Merlin after their trip to Antarctica.

Peep.

Kathleen picked up Penny and held the little penguin in her arms.

Peep. Peep.

Jack and Annie laughed. "How are you, Penny?" asked Jack.

"She is wonderful," said Morgan. "She is dearly loved in Camelot. I would say Penny has become the very heart of our kingdom."

"She hasn't gotten any bigger," said Jack.

Merlin smiled. "Time passes very slowly in Camelot," he said.

"Indeed," said Morgan. "Camelot has hardly aged at all since we last saw you."

"But you have accomplished much in that time," said Merlin. "You have completed your missions to help four artists give their gifts to the world."

"And from all we hear," said Morgan, "you were as successful with Charles Dickens as you were with Lady Augusta Gregory, Louis Armstrong, and Wolfgang Amadeus Mozart."

"I guess we were," Jack said modestly.

"I loved Charles," said Annie. "I loved all of them. I felt like we became good friends with them."

"Yeah, and I'm really sad that I won't see them again," said Jack.

"We thought you might feel that way," said Kathleen.

"Merlin and Morgan have something to show you," said Teddy.

"But first, may we have the magic violin and bow back?" asked Kathleen.

"Oh, sure," said Jack. He reached into his backpack and pulled out the violin and bow.

Teddy took the violin from him, and Kathleen took the bow. "On your last four missions, you played a magic violin, a magic Irish whistle, a magic trumpet, and a magic flute," said Kathleen.

Jack and Annie nodded.

"Do you remember where the magic came from?" said Kathleen. She tossed the violin bow into the air. It was still for a moment. Then it began to twirl around and around. There was a flash of blue light. The violin and bow disappeared. Floating in the air was an object shaped like the spiraled horn of a unicorn.

"The Wand of Dianthus!" Jack and Annie said together.

"Yes," said Kathleen. She plucked the wand from the air and handed it to Merlin.

Merlin closed his eyes. He waved the Wand

of Dianthus in a circle and whispered words Jack couldn't understand.

There was a *whoosh* of wind, and they were all standing at the corner of Jack and Annie's street. Some people were walking by in the dusk. Jack looked worriedly at Merlin, Morgan, Teddy, Kathleen, and Penny. What would people say when they saw them?

"Do not worry," Morgan said, as if she could read Jack's mind. "They see and hear only you and Annie."

"Listen carefully," said Merlin.

Jack listened. Beautiful music was coming from a house on the corner.

"A string quartet is rehearsing for a Mozart concert at a church this Saturday," said Merlin.

"Oh, wow," said Annie.

Merlin waved the wand in a circle and whispered more magic words.

Whoosh! They were all standing outside a window of a large brick building. Inside, kids were playing trumpets, saxophones, and drums. "Hey, it's the band room at the middle school," Jack said.

"Yes, the band is rehearsing a Louis Armstrong song for the jazz festival next week," said Morgan.

Again Merlin waved the wand in a circle and whispered magic words. *Whoosh!* They all stood at a window of a white wooden building. "It's the Frog Creek library!" said Annie. Inside the library, a woman sat in an armchair, talking and waving her hands. Children sat at her feet, listening.

"A storyteller is telling Irish folktales," said Kathleen. "Stories collected by Augusta Gregory."

Merlin waved the wand in a circle and whispered magic words again. *Whoosh!* They were all standing at the back of a dark auditorium. Actors were rehearsing on the stage.

"Back by popular demand," Teddy whispered, "the Frog Creek Little Theater presents Charles Dickens's *A Christmas Carol*."

"Yay! We can go see it again," whispered Annie.

"Yes. And that is how you will visit with

Charles Dickens again," said Merlin.

"Charles Dickens, Lady Augusta Gregory, Louis Armstrong, Wolfgang Amadeus Mozart, and all other great artists live on through their work," said Morgan.

"You put your four friends on the path to giving their gifts to the world," said Kathleen.

"And the world *still* receives their gifts," said Teddy.

"You accomplished your mission," Merlin said to Jack and Annie. "Thank you for helping bring happiness to millions."

"You're welcome," said Jack.

"No problem," said Annie.

Jack turned back to watch the rehearsal of *A Christmas Carol*.

The Ghost of Christmas Future had just left the stage, and Scrooge was alone in his bedroom. The actor playing Scrooge started hopping about, laughing and crying in the same breath. "I am as light as a feather!" he shouted. "I am as happy as an angel!"

Jack and Annie laughed at Scrooge's wild joy. Jack turned around to laugh with the others. But they were gone. Merlin, Morgan, Teddy, Kathleen, and Penny had all vanished.

"Where . . . ?" Jack said.

"They must've gone home to Camelot," said Annie. "But I'll bet we'll see them again soon."

Jack nodded. "We should go home now, too," he said.

As Scrooge was shouting "Merry Christmas!" to the world, Jack and Annie slipped out of the Frog Creek Little Theater. Then they ran through the cool autumn evening, heading for home.

More Facts About Charles Dickens

In the autumn of 1843, the young writer Charles Dickens was greatly disturbed by the plight of England's poor people. He was especially worried about children, as he was haunted by his own memories of being a desperately poor child. Seeking guidance and inspiration, he often took twilight walks through some of London's worst neighborhoods.

One evening on a walk, Dickens came up with the idea of writing *A Christmas Carol in Prose: Being a Ghost Story of Christmas*, as he subtitled it. The story included a miserly man named Scrooge, a small child known as Tiny Tim, and three Christmas ghosts. Dickens wrote feverishly and finished his ghost story by early December. It was quickly published and sold out its first six thousand copies.

A Christmas Carol has since become one of the world's best-loved stories. Written at a time when Christmas traditions were on the decline, it is often credited with reviving holiday customs and encouraging families to gather together during the Christmas season and to be more generous toward those less fortunate.

After writing *A Christmas Carol*, Charles Dickens went on to create many other great works, including *David Copperfield*, *Bleak House*, and *Great Expectations*. During the Victorian age, his books not only brought people great pleasure, but helped inspire Britain to make many reforms to improve conditions for the poor.

Fun Activities for Jack and Annie and *You*!

Light the Way

In *A Ghost Tale for Christmas Time*, Jack and Annie learn that sometimes people need friends to show them the way. Make this festive lantern to give to a friend and light up their day!

You will need:

- Colored tissue paper
- Ruler
- Scissors
- Water
- Glue
- Bowl
- Clean glass jar
- Small paintbrush
- Glitter (optional)
- Wide ribbon
- Battery-operated night-light or tea candle

1. Cut the tissue paper into small squares, about one inch by one inch.

2. Mix a small amount of water into the glue in a disposable or easy-to-clean bowl.

3. Brush the watered-down glue onto the outside of the glass jar with the paintbrush, starting at the top and doing small sections of the jar at a time.

4. Press the tissue-paper squares onto the glue on the jar. You can alternate between colors to make a pattern, or choose a design of your own.

5. After all the squares have been placed on the jar, you can use the regular glue that has not been watered down to decorate with glitter. Let dry.

6. Add regular glue to the rim of the jar. Wrap the ribbon around the rim and tie it in a bow. Let dry.

7. Place a night-light inside the jar or ask an adult to place a tea candle inside. Remember to never leave a burning candle unattended. Enjoy the colorful light of your very own lantern!

Puzzle of the Three Ghosts

Jack and Annie learned a lot about Charles Dickens on their adventure in London. Answer the following questions to put your knowledge of *A Ghost Tale for Christmas Time* to the test.

You can use a notebook or make a copy of this page if you don't want to write in your book.

1. Jack and Annie are supposed to clean a

_ _ _ _ _ _ _.

☐ ◯ ☐ ☐ ☐ ☐ ☐

2. Charles Dickens is visited by three

_ _ _ _ _ _.

☐ ☐ ☐ ◯ ☐ ☐

3. Mr. Pinch uses the phrase "Bah, _ _ _ _ _ _!

☐ ☐ ☐ ☐ ☐ ◯

4. Charles Dickens's father was sent to debtors'

_ _ _ _ _ _.

☐ ☐ ◯ ☐ ☐ ☐

5. Jack's bag was this color.

☐ ☐ ☐ ☐ ○

6. Annie helps the magic by _ _ _ _ _ _ _.

☐ ☐ ☐ ☐ ○ ☐ ☐

7. Jack plays this musical instrument.

☐ ☐ ☐ ○ ☐ ☐

8. The chimney sweeps are named Harry and _ _ _ _ _.

☐ ☐ ○ ☐ ☐

Now look at your answers above. The letters that are circled spell a word—but that word is scrambled! Can you unscramble the letters to complete the final puzzle?

People in England use a different kind of money than us. In Charles Dickens's time, one of their coins was called a _ _ _ _ _ _ _ _.

Here's a special preview of
Magic Tree House® Fact Tracker
Rags and Riches: Kids in the Time
of Charles Dickens

After meeting Charles Dickens, Jack and Annie
wanted to find out more about him and kids in
his time. Track down the facts with them!

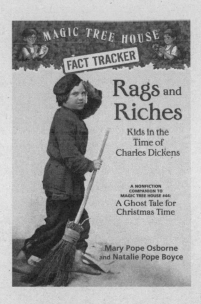

Available now!

1

Hard Times for Kids

In the 1800s, England was a very powerful country. The city of London was the largest, richest city in the world. Signs of the city's wealth were everywhere. Parks, stores, factories, and beautiful buildings filled the city. Down by the wharves, hundreds of workers built ships that sailed all over the world. Factories ran night and day, turning out things like cloth, beer, furniture, and watches. London was growing, and the number of people in the city was growing as well. New buildings seemed to go up overnight. As the city grew, many people made money and lived very well.

But there was another side of London. While the city was rich, it was also poor. Terrible slums stood only blocks away from beautiful mansions. While some people ate at fancy restaurants, others were hungry, homeless, and sick. As wealthy children visited parks or museums, gangs of poor children roamed the streets, selling anything they could find, and sometimes even stealing. Why was life so hard for these children? What caused such terrible poverty in this rich city?

The Industrial Revolution
For thousands of years, most people in England lived in the country. Children grew up on farms and in small villages. They

worked alongside their parents on their farms or in village shops. Parents treated them like little adults. Even though children worked hard, they were with their families or other people they knew.

This country life changed in the late 1700s. The *Industrial Revolution* had begun in England. Much of the old way of

Industrial is a word that refers to work done by machinery in factories. **Revolution** is a change that happens quickly.

England was the first country to have lots of factories.

life came to an end, and things were never the same again.

The Industrial Revolution started around 1790 and lasted until the early 1900s. The discovery of steam engines helped to start it. In the past, factories used river water to power their machines. Steam engines made it possible to build factories anywhere, not just next to rivers.

Factories and mills sprang up in towns and cities all over England. Thousands of people left the countryside hoping to find work in them.

Trains Speed Things Up
For most of the 1800s, there were no cars. People walked or used horses and boats to get around. Traveling anywhere took a lot of time. This problem was solved by steam-

powered trains. They made it possible to
get places quickly. A trip that used to take
days could now be made in hours.

Person walking fast = 4 miles per hour

Horse-drawn carriage = 10 miles per hour

Trains = 30-40 miles per hour

By 1854, thousands of miles of train track connected cities and towns to one another. Trains became the most popular way to travel and to ship products from the factories. Trains puffed in and out of London night and day, carrying hundreds of people.

Industrial Revolution

Steam engine

New factories everywhere

People move from the country

Trains

Don't miss

Magic Tree House® #45
(A Merlin Mission)
A Crazy Day with Cobras

**Jack and Annie are whisked back to India,
where they must face venomous king cobras
to help save a friend!**

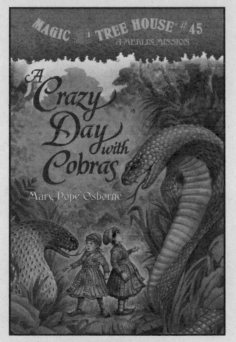

Available now!

Help Jack and Annie on their important mission for Merlin!

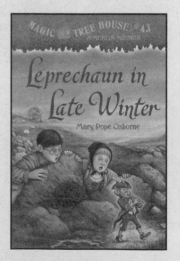

Have you read all of the Magic Tree House® books?

Merlin Missions

Plus Magic Tree House® Fact Trackers
and more! For a full list of titles, visit
MagicTreeHouse.com

BRING MAGIC TREE HOUSE TO YOUR SCHOOL!

Magic Tree House musicals now available for performance by young people!

Ask your teacher or director
to contact
Music Theatre International
for more information:
**BroadwayJr.com
Licensing@MTIshows.com
(212) 541-4684**

MAGIC TREE HOUSE COLLECTION

DINOSAURS BEFORE DARK KIDS

MAGIC TREE HOUSE COLLECTION

The Knight at Dawn KIDS

ATTENTION, TEACHERS!

The Magic Tree House **CLASSROOM ADVENTURES PROGRAM** is a free, comprehensive set of online educational resources for teachers developed by Mary Pope Osborne as a gift to teachers, to thank them for their enthusiastic support of the series. Educators can learn more at MTHClassroomAdventures.org.

MAGIC TREE HOUSE